SOPHIE the SNOOP

Finding the right name isn't easy!
See what else Sophie tries out....

1: SOPHIE the AWESOME

2: SOPHIE the HERO

3: SOPHIE the CHATTERBOX

4: SOPHIE the ZILLIONAIRE

5: SOPHIE the SNOOP

6: SOPHIE the DAREDEVIL

7: SOPHIE the SWEETHEART

SOPHIE the SNOOP

by Lara Bergen

illustrated by Laura Tallardy

SCHOLASTIC INC.

New York Toronto London Auckland
Sydney Mexico City New Delhi Hong Kong

For Parker

If you purchased this book without a cover, you should be aware that this book is stolen property. It was reported as "unsold and destroyed" to the publisher, and neither the author nor the publisher has received any payment for this "stripped book."

No part of this publication may be reproduced, stored in a retrieval system, or transmitted in any form or by any means, electronic, mechanical, photocopying, recording, or otherwise, without written permission of the publisher. For information regarding permission, write to Scholastic Inc., Attention: Permissions Department, 557 Broadway, New York, NY 10012.

ISBN 978-0-545-26483-9

Text copyright © 2011 by Lara Bergen
Illustrations copyright © 2011 by Scholastic Inc.
All rights reserved. Published by Scholastic Inc.
SCHOLASTIC and associated logos are trademarks
and/or registered trademarks of Scholastic Inc.

12 11 10 9 8 7 6 5 4 3 2   11 12 13 14 15 16/0

Printed in the U.S.A.   40
First printing, April 2011
Designed by Tim Hall

CHAPTER 1

What a day! Sophie thought.

Because today was the day she was *something*. And that something was Sophie the *Snoop*.

Yes! That was who she was from now on.

More than anything, Sophie wanted to be extra-special. To be extra-great at . . . *something*. She had tried to be great at *everything* at first. But that was hard. So then she had tried to be great at one thing. Like being a hero. Or being honest. Or being rich. But that was hard, too.

Then, suddenly, it came to her in a great big

whoosh. Sophie was great at solving mysteries. She was a natural snoop!

First she solved the Missing Horse Bank Mystery, just like that. (The thief had been her little brother, Max.)

Then she solved the Mystery of the Missing Business Cards. (Of course, that wasn't really a mystery. *Sophie* had taken her dad's cards. But he never would have found them without her. That was a fact.)

Now Sophie the Snoop could not wait to solve her next case—whatever it was!

So she was very ready when her mom called out, "It's almost time to go to school. Hey! Who left the toilet seat up?"

Sophie tiptoed to the downstairs bathroom— the scene of the crime. (She knew that snoops tiptoed, so she had to. But she did it very fast.)

"This is a case for Sophie the Snoop, Mom!" she cried.

Sophie looked around the bathroom and found a clue almost right away. It was the mug she had painted for her dad's birthday. She picked it up off the sink.

"Aha!" she said.

Sophie flashed her mom a big smile and headed for the kitchen. Her dad was waiting by the toaster for something to pop up. Sophie tiptoed up behind him and shouted, "Gotcha!"

Her dad turned, surprised, and saw the mug. He sighed and held up his hands. "Sure enough. That's my kitten mug. Guilty as charged," he told her.

Sophie smiled. She crossed her arms. "I knew it! No case is too tough for Sophie the Snoop!" she declared.

She did not even try to tell her dad that the picture on the mug was not really of Tiptoe the kitten. It was of *him.* (She should know. She had painted it. Oh, well. That was okay. She was not Sophie the *Artist*, after all.)

Sophie's mom walked up behind her. She gave Sophie's shoulder a soft squeeze. "Good work, Sherlock Holmes."

Sophie felt proud. But also puzzled. "Who's Sherlock Holmes?" she had to ask.

"Who's Sherlock Holmes?" her dad repeated. "Why, he's only one of the greatest detectives ever. Remember? I dressed up like him for Halloween last year?"

Sophie was still confused.

"Sherlock Holmes was the English guy with the hat and the magnifying glass," her dad went on. "You know— 'Elementary, my dear Watson!'" he said with a funny accent. It was British, Sophie thought.

Sophie had to giggle. But she nodded, too. Yep. She remembered the hat. It had a brim on the front *and* the back.

So one of the greatest detectives ever wore it, huh? Sophie thought about that for a minute.

Then she thought about the box in the basement. The one with "Costumes" written on the side. Was the hat in there?

She left her parents in the kitchen. And she tiptoed downstairs to find out!

Ugh, Sophie thought as she reached the bottom of the basement stairs. This was not going to be an easy job—even for a snoop as great as Sophie! The basement was not just full of boxes—it was full of all kinds of stuff.

There was stuff like old baby toys that even two-year-old Max had outgrown, her dad's dusty drum set, and exactly forty-one silver trophies. They all belonged to Sophie's mom. (Sophie did not know why she kept them all the way down there. If they were *Sophie's* trophies, they'd be in the living room, on display!)

Sophie sighed and looked all around. She had to find that costume box somehow. But where should she start?

She tiptoed around very slowly, just like a snoop should. Then she saw bins full of lights and Christmas ornaments. Next to those was a stack of Easter baskets. Plus a bag of pink plastic grass.

Is there more holiday stuff there? Sophie wondered.

She poked around. Yes! There were the

cauldrons for trick-or-treat candy. The plastic tombstones for the front yard. A sack of fake spiderwebs. *Oh!* And the brain-shaped Jell-O mold.

And there was also the costume box!

Sophie pumped her fist. *Bingo!* Sophie the Snoop had done it again.

She yanked off the lid and dug in.

She tossed aside the princess dresses and cat ears and fairy wings. Then she came to the Batman suit she had worn when she was four. (What had she been thinking?!) She dropped it on the floor.

Next she pulled out a whole stack of hats—fireman, wizard, cowboy, and more. She was getting closer! Then, at last, at the very bottom, she found the Sherlock Holmes hat she was looking for.

She smiled and put it on.

The hat was big. And kind of itchy. Sophie was not sure which side was the front. She wondered why Sherlock Holmes had picked it. But if one of the greatest detectives ever wore it, Sophie the Snoop would, too.

Then Sophie spotted something else in the costume box. The big magnifying glass! She guessed that great detectives had to solve *all* mysteries...no matter how small.

She picked up the magnifying glass and looked at her hand under it. She saw lines she'd never seen before!

She felt something tickle her ankle. She jumped, then looked down. It was Tiptoe, her kitten.

"Tiptoe! Let me look at you!" she said.

Hey, what a great name for a snoop's pet! she thought.

She knelt down and held the magnifying glass to Tiptoe's nose. Then she looked at her ears and her eyes and the tiny pads on her toes.

In fact, once Sophie started, she could not stop looking at everything up close!

Suddenly, Sophie heard a sound. It was coming from upstairs.

"SOPHIE!"

Sophie almost answered. But then she stopped. Her mom was not calling her *whole* name. She was Sophie the *Snoop*, after all!

She rubbed Tiptoe's chin and waited.

Then Sophie heard something else: "Sophie Hamm Miller! Where are you? You're going to miss the bus!"

Uh-oh! That was not the whole name Sophie had hoped to hear. But she knew she'd better go.

She'd be in trouble if she didn't. That was no mystery at all!

CHAPTER 2

Sophie tiptoed up to the bus stop just in time. The school bus was rolling down the street.

"Cool hat!" said her best friend, Kate Barry, when she saw Sophie.

"Why, thank you!" Sophie said back. (She tried to say it with an English accent. But she wasn't sure it came out right. At all.)

Then Sophie held up the magnifying glass in front of her eye. "And how were your blueberry pancakes this morning?" she asked.

Kate's mouth fell open. "How did you know?"

Sophie grinned. "Elementary, my dear Kate.

Your lips are purple. And there's syrup on your shirt."

Kate quickly licked her lips — and the syrup off her shirt. Then she climbed onto the bus behind Sophie.

"Hey, why are you tiptoeing?" Kate asked.

Sophie led Kate to their favorite seat, all the way in the back. "Because I'm a snoop, and snoops tiptoe," she said. "Everyone knows that."

Then Sophie told Kate all about her new name.

"Sophie the Snoop...I like it!" Kate said.

Kate was so great! Sophie hugged her.

"There's just one thing," Kate added. "I get the tiptoeing. But do you really have to talk like that?"

Was Kate talking about her British accent?

"You don't like it?" Sophie asked.

Kate twisted her mouth and shrugged.

Sophie shrugged, too. "Okay," she said in her normal voice. That was a lot easier, anyway. Besides, snoops solved mysteries. What did it matter how they talked?

Sophie just hoped everyone else would like her name as much as Kate did. Then they could call her Sophie the Snoop instead of boring Sophie M. But first she needed to solve more mysteries! So she made an announcement as soon as she got to room 10.

"Sophie the Snoop, at your service!" she said. "There is no mystery I can't solve!"

"Is that why you're wearing that funny hat?" Dean asked.

Funny? Sophie straightened it. "For your information, this is the hat the world's greatest detectives wear," she said.

"Oh, yeah? I don't think so." Grace shook her head. "Nancy Drew is the world's greatest detective. And she never wears funny hats."

Sophie frowned. She did not know too much about Nancy Drew. But she bet if she'd had a hat like Sophie's, she would have worn it, too.

"All I'm saying is I solve mysteries. That's what I do," Sophie said.

Sydney got a worried look. "Do we have to pay you?" she asked.

Sophie guessed that Sydney remembered how she'd tried to get rich the other day. She had helped her friends, but only if they paid her.

"Nope," Sophie told Sydney. "My mystery-solving is all free!"

"Hey! I've got a mystery," Toby Myers said suddenly.

Sophie turned to him. Toby? He was the *last* person she thought would speak up.

Not that Toby couldn't have a mystery. Anyone could! It was just that Toby never talked to Sophie. At least not anymore.

From preschool until last year, Toby and Sophie had been best friends. (In fact, Sophie remembered that back when they were four, they had *both* been Batman for Halloween.) But now Toby hung out with yucky Archie Dolan. And the fact was he was just not the same anymore. But that was fine with Sophie—now she had Kate.

But maybe Toby was changing back.

(Somewhere way down deep inside her, Sophie always kind of hoped he might.)

"What's your mystery?" she asked him with a big grin.

Toby started to laugh. "Who cut the cheese?" he yelled.

That was when Archie walked up and gave him a high five.

Sophie's eyes got hot. She crossed her arms and turned away. And the hope she'd had that Toby might change? She pushed it way down deep inside her again.

In the meantime, Kate stepped up. "That's no mystery, Toby," she said. "Everyone knows *you* cut the cheese!"

Ha! Kate really was great.

The other kids laughed. Sophie grinned and let out a big breath.

Just then, Ms. Moffly waved to them from behind her desk. Sophie thought her dress looked extra-pretty that day. But her hair was kind of a mess.

"Class! Let's get started," Ms. Moffly called. Then she blew her nose. "But first, who can tell me who this homework belongs to?"

Ms. Moffly held up a math worksheet. Someone had forgotten to sign his or her name. She waited for an answer, but all she got were shrugs and "Not me's."

Suddenly, Sophie realized something. Her first case of the school day had just popped up!

"Ms. Moffly! Ms. Moffly!" she cried. "This is a case for me, Sophie the Snoop!"

Sophie pulled out her magnifying glass. Then she tiptoed up to the teacher's desk. She held out her hand. "Now I will examine the evidence," she said.

Ms. Moffly smiled and handed the worksheet over. Sophie could tell she was glad for the help. Ms. Moffly was pretty good at teaching times tables. And she was not bad at all at reading out loud. But she was no detective. They probably did not teach that at teacher school. That was too bad.

"Okay." Sophie studied the paper. She recognized the math problems they had done the night before. "Aha!" she said. "A clue: Look at all this eraser stuff!"

"Does that tell you something?" Ms. Moffly asked. Sophie thought she looked very impressed.

"Sure!" Sophie said. "It tells me that this homework belongs to someone who has a pink eraser. And who changes their mind a lot."

Then Sophie pointed to a spot on the paper. It looked like gravy. Or chocolate. Or mud. "And see this?" she asked Ms. Moffly. "This tells me that whoever this paper belongs to is a big slob."

Ms. Moffly sighed and nodded. "Yes. I see that a lot."

"Of course, the real clue is the handwriting," Sophie went on. "So here's what we do. Have everyone do their homework again, and I'll compare those worksheets to this one."

Ms. Moffly clicked her tongue. "Mmm, I don't know, Sophie. I'm not sure we have time for that."

Sophie shrugged. "Well...okay. Then I guess

I'll have to work with what we've got," she said. She turned to the blackboard and picked up some chalk. "So, what do we know?"

The Case of the Unsigned Homework

Clue #1 — The suspect uses a pink eraser.

Clue #2 — The suspect eats gravy, chocolate, or mud.

Clue #3 — The suspect writes numbers like this: 1, 2, 3.

All of a sudden, Sophie stopped.

She looked at her **3**. And her **2**. And her **1**.

Then she thought about the pink eraser on her pencil. And the chocolate chip cookies she had eaten the night before . . . at the very same time she was doing her homework.

Then Sophie looked at the homework paper. Yep. Those looked like the same answers — exactly — that she had gotten.

Sophie put the paper down. She wrote her

18

name at the top. Then she handed it back to Ms. Moffly. "Um, here, Ms. Moffly. Case closed."

Ms. Moffly smiled and patted Sophie on the hat. "Good work, Sophie the Snoop."

☆　　☆　　☆

Okay. So the Case of the Unsigned Homework wasn't the greatest mystery in the world. But it was something, at least. *Bring on the next one!* Sophie thought.

The only thing was that the next mystery did not come. Suddenly, it was three o'clock. School was over, and no more cases had popped up.

That was the problem with school, Sophie guessed. No rich people ever got kidnapped. And no jewels ever got robbed. But still. What good was being a snoop if there was nothing to snoop . . . at all?

Sophie wondered if Sherlock Holmes had felt the same way when he was in school.

"Hey, I have a mystery," Kate said as they tiptoed to the bus together.

Hooray! It was about time!

"What is it?" Sophie asked.

"Where are all the mysteries?" Kate said, laughing.

Sophie grinned. But she also rolled her eyes.

"Hey! Maybe something will happen at soccer practice," Kate went on. "Maybe someone will kidnap the coach!"

Sophie nodded. Probably not...

But she could always hope.

CHAPTER 3

Soccer was a new thing for Sophie. She had just started playing that year.

She had wanted to do something after school. But she hadn't been sure what. (Just as long as it wasn't ballet. Her sister, Hayley, did enough of that for both of them.)

Then Kate told Sophie about soccer. She had played the year before.

So Sophie's mom signed her up, too.

So far, it was pretty fun, though Sophie thought it would be more fun if her ball didn't always try to roll away. At practice, she was always chasing it while everyone else played.

It would also be nice if her feet would listen to her—for once. Did they think it was funny when she tried to kick and missed the ball?

Sophie did not.

What Sophie liked best about soccer were the uniforms. They were the best color—sour-apple green! And the girls on her team were all super-nice. Plus Coach Courtney was great. Especially when she said things like "Good job, Sophie! You're getting better every week!"

That day Coach Courtney said something else, though. Something not as great. That day she said, "Sophie, what's with all this running on your toes? Do you think you could stop? And that's a pretty cool hat. But you can't wear it while you play, you know."

Oh.

Actually, maybe those were good things after all. Tiptoe soccer was not easy. And Sophie's detective hat was making her head sweat a lot.

Plus no matter how many times she pushed it back, it kept sliding down to her nose.

Sophie ran over to the sideline, where the girls kept their soccer bags. They all looked the same and were labeled "Official"—which was pretty cool, Sophie thought.

Sophie picked up her bag and dropped her hat inside. Her magnifying glass was already there. Plus a notebook. And a pencil. Just in case there was a soccer mystery. A snoop had to be ready, after all!

She spotted her water bottle on the grass. She picked it up and took a long sip. Then she slipped it into her bag, pulled the drawstring tight, and ran back onto the field.

To start, the team did some drills. They kicked the ball with both sides of their feet. Then they had dribbling races. (And for the first time, Sophie beat Kate!)

After that, Coach Courtney handed out big, bright orange tank tops to half the girls.

It was time to play a real game!

"Can I be goalie?" Sophie asked. Not because she liked to block the ball, but because then she wouldn't have to run around as much.

During her time in goal, Sophie only let the ball by twice. That was good for her! Then her turn was over. It was time to run back and forth across the field. Sophie got the ball and took a shot...and *wow!* She scored!

Or—no. She *would* have scored—if she hadn't shot the ball into her own team's goal.

"Sorry," she told her teammates.

She would never be named Sophie the Soccer Star. That was for sure.

Finally—hooray!—Coach Courtney called, "Water break, girls!" But Sophie was too tired to drink. She lay down in the grass and took a giant breath instead.

"Sophie! *Sophie!*" Kate was calling her name.

Sophie looked up and saw Kate pulling a girl named Ana by the hand across the field.

"Tell her, Ana! Tell Sophie what's wrong!" Kate said.

"It's my water bottle. I can't find it anywhere," Ana said, shrugging.

The Case of the Missing Water Bottle!

Sophie forgot all about being tired. She jumped to her feet. "This sounds like a case for Sophie the Snoop!" she cried.

"See!" Kate grinned. "I told you, Ana."

Ana nodded at Sophie. "I'm really thirsty! Can you hurry?" she asked.

"I will do my best," Sophie told her. "There might be witnesses. But first, I need the facts. Where did you last see your water bottle? And did you notice anyone out of the ordinary or *suspicious* around?"

Ana pointed to the sideline. "The last time I saw my water bottle, it was there. And what do you mean by 'out of the ordinary'? Do you mean like you before, when you were wearing that funny hat?"

Funny? My hat?

Sophie started to shake her head. But speaking of hats, Sophie wasn't sure if she needed hers to crack this case. But she did need her notepad and magnifying glass!

Sophie nodded back toward the sideline. "Come on. Follow me."

She tiptoed—again—as fast as she could across the grass and picked up her bag.

No, wait. That was Kate's. Sophie picked up another. It was heavier, and it had her name on the side. Perfect. She reached in and pulled out her notepad and a pencil.

She carefully wrote The Case of the Missing Water Bottle.

Then she looked up at Ana and got ready to list the clues.

"So what does your water bottle look like, exactly?" Sophie asked. "Give me every detail. Don't leave anything out."

"Well . . ." Ana twisted her braids as she thought. "It's metal." She paused. "And it's silver, but not shiny. It's kind of dull. The top is black. And you twist it off. Oh! And it has two black swooshes on the sides. You know?"

Sophie nodded as she wrote everything down. "Yeah, I think I do. It sounds kind of like my bottle."

Then Sophie stopped writing.

Hold on.

That sounded a *lot* like her water bottle. Except for the two-swoosh part. Sophie's bottle used to have two swooshes, but then the dishwasher washed one off.

Slowly, Sophie bent down. She picked her bag up again, reached in, and felt around.

Whoops.

Sure enough, there were two bottles inside. Sophie pulled out both. She handed the one with two swooshes to Ana.

Kate raised an arm in triumph. "See! I knew she would find it, Ana!"

"Sorry, Ana," Sophie said, making a face. "I picked yours up by mistake, I guess."

Ana smiled. "That's okay. I'm just glad to have it back." She took a very short drink. "There's, uh, not much left."

Whoops. Again.

"Yeah . . . I guess I drank most of it. Sorry about that, too," Sophie said.

Tweeeet! Coach Courtney blew her whistle.

"Back on the field, girls!" she yelled.

"Here, Ana, take my bottle." Sophie traded with Ana and they ran back onto the field.

Sophie was glad that another case was solved, at least. But if someone *else* could be guilty the next time . . . that would be a nice change!

The next day, Sophie's wish came true. There was a brand-new mystery at school. And Sophie was pretty sure that it did not involve her.

It was the Case of the Missing Ms. Moffly!

Because Sophie's third-grade class had a substitute.

"Where do you think she is?" some kids whispered as they hung up their coats.

"This is *definitely* a case for Sophie the Snoop!" Sophie declared. Then she whipped out a spy kit she had put together at home. A real spy kit, just like every snoop should own!

Not only did she have her notebook and magnifying glass, now she had little plastic bags for collecting evidence, too. And her mom's rubber gloves, to make sure she did not mess up any fingerprints. Fingerprints were a great way to find criminals. Everyone knew that. So Sophie also had baby powder and a small paintbrush and a roll of clear tape. She had learned that they could pick up fingerprints (though she hadn't tried it yet).

Plus she had a juicy lemon — otherwise known as invisible ink! All you had to do was write with the juice. When it dried, you could not see a thing. But if you left the paper in the sun, the message magically appeared.

Finally, she had 3-D glasses from a movie she had seen. They weren't exactly night-vision goggles. Those would have been the best. But these were better than nothing, she guessed.

But before Sophie could even flip open her notebook to crack her latest case, the substitute spoke up. "Um...good morning, class. If you're wondering where Ms. Moffly is, I'm afraid she's sick today. So I'll be your substitute. If you all could . . . um . . . sit down, please."

Oh, great.

Sophie put down her notebook. She plopped her chin into her hands. Why did the sub have to *tell* them that Ms. Moffly was home sick? Sophie *so* could have figured that out, she bet!

The substitute, meanwhile, turned to the board. She wrote her name in big letters that sloped to one side.

"Um . . . my name is Ms. Steele," she said. She took a deep breath and turned back around.

Sophie studied her. She looked younger than Ms. Moffly. And she was taller, too. She was not wearing much makeup. Her face was plain and thin. And she sure knew how to spoil mysteries! Sophie would just have to wait for the *next* one to roll around. Oh, well.

Luckily, she had a new mystery to solve pretty soon.

It was the Mystery of What's Up with Ms. Steele!

Why did she seem so *nervous*?

And why was she so *mean*?

And why did so many things she said sound like questions? What was up with that, anyway?

Sophie had had lots of substitutes before. But none like this.

Of course, Sophie had no problem with the sub telling Toby and Archie to sit down.

And "no gum in school" was a rule Ms. Moffly also had. (Too bad.)

Then there was what Ms. Steele said to Mindy VonBoffmann. Mindy hardly ever got in trouble. She was usually too busy tattling on other kids.

"Um...you there...in the pink shirt. Is that a *phone* in your hand? It looks very nice, but could you please put it away? Um...right now?" Ms. Steele said.

Sophie watched as Mindy looked up, wide-eyed. She *did* have a phone in her hand. It was very pink and very shiny.

"What? This? Oh! Don't worry, it's not *real*!" Mindy told the teacher. Then Mindy smiled and flipped it open. "See? It has lip gloss inside." She pulled out the antenna brush and dabbed some gloss all around her mouth.

Ooh! Sophie stared. *A lip-gloss phone! Cool!* She had never seen one of them. She hated wanting things that Mindy had. But sometimes she just had to.

"Um . . . I'm sorry . . . ," Ms. Steele said.

Mindy smiled. "Oh, that's okay."

". . . but you *still* have to put it away," Ms. Steele continued.

Mindy's shiny lips fell open. Her eyebrows made a bitter V as she put the phone in her cubby.

Sophie smiled a tiny smile. Yes, that was fine. Definitely. But other things the sub did were not okay.

Like when Ms. Steele saw Ben's stuffed Tweety Bird and made him put it away. That was so unfair. Ms. Moffly always let him keep it at his desk. It was Ben's very favorite thing.

And talk about unfair—next the sub told Sophie to take off her detective hat!

"But Ms. Moffly let me wear it yesterday. All day. Except for the Pledge of Allegiance." Sophie took a breath. "She also lets Ben keep Tweety Bird at his desk," she added.

"Well . . ." The sub bit her lip. "Um... I guess I'm not Ms. Moffly?" she said.

Sophie sighed and pulled her hat off. "You don't have to be a detective to figure *that* out," she muttered to Kate.

She did not mean for Ms. Steele to hear her. But—*oops!*—she did. And so did the rest of the class. Everyone started laughing. That was when the sub got very red.

"Okay. Okay. That's enough!" she said. She pointed to Sophie. "Um... you. Sophie? Switch seats with him?"

Sophie watched where she pointed next—at Dean. Her stomach did a backflip. Dean sat next to Toby. That meant now *she* had to sit next to him!

Sophie had not sat next to Toby for more than a second since last year. How would she do it for five hours?

She walked slowly to his table. Then she sat down and scooted her chair as far away from him as she could.

"Solve any mysteries yet today, *Snoop*?" Toby asked. Then he snickered. And burped.

Sophie scooted even farther away. She was *so* glad when it was time for gym and she could get away from him! They played Sharks and Minnows outside.

Or most of them did.

Sophie and Kate mostly stood at the edge of the field and talked about how they could not wait for the day to end.

"You know what we should do?" Sophie said.

"What? Pretend to be sick? And get our moms to take us home?" Kate asked.

Sophie shook her head. "No. When we get back to room ten, we should write each other notes!"

Kate grinned. But then she raised her eyebrow a little bit. "I bet 'no notes in school' is a big rule for Ms. Steele," she said.

"Aha!" Sophie held up one finger. "But I have a lemon!"

Kate looked at her blankly. "I don't get it," she said.

Sophie leaned over and whispered, "We can use invisible ink! Lemon juice ink stays invisible until you leave it out in the sun. If Ms. Steele sees the paper, she won't even know it's a note."

"Cool!" Kate nodded. But then she rubbed her chin. "But if we're inside all day, how are *we* going to read the notes?"

Oh.

Kate had a good point. She always did.

Suddenly, Mr. Hurley, the gym teacher, hollered at them: "Hey! You minnows! Start swimming, or you're automatically it!"

Quickly, Kate and Sophie dashed across the field. No sharks caught them. *Phew!* They stopped to catch their breath.

"Hey, I have an idea! Let's write *code* notes," Kate said.

Code notes? *Yes!* Sophie clapped her hands.

What a snoopy idea! It was just like invisible ink—except you didn't need the sun.

"Let's use the code where numbers stand for the letters," Sophie suggested.

"You mean one for 'A' and two for 'B,' like that?" Kate asked.

Sophie nodded. "And we can leave them in a certain spot—like the corner of our desk. Then we give a secret signal so the other person knows to pick it up!"

"Sounds good!" Kate said. "But what kind of secret signal?" she asked.

Sophie shrugged. "How about this? *Whooo.*" She made an owl sound.

"Hmm . . ." Kate watched the other kids running around, tagging each other. She shook her head. "I don't know. That might sound kind of weird in the classroom. How about a sneeze?"

Sophie tried it out: *"A-choo!"*

"Bless you!" Mr. Hurley hollered over to her. "Now get back in there and swim, swim, *swim*, you two minnows!"

When gym was over, the class went back to room 10. As they walked in, Sophie noticed that Ms. Steele looked nervous, still.

"Um...please get out your spelling books, class?" she said to them.

Sophie went to her cubby to get her book, along with everybody else. Then she started to head back to Toby's table. She *almost* didn't even mind it. She was much too busy thinking about what kind of code note to write to Kate. Maybe something about how gross Toby was . . .

And he'd never know what it said! That was the best part.

Suddenly, a screechy voice rang out. It made Sophie's ears hurt. It also made her heart leap— all the way up to her throat.

The voice belonged to Mindy. And she was saying, "Someone stole my phone!"

At last—a real mystery!

The Case of the Missing Phone!

Well, *lip-gloss* phone. But that was even better, in Sophie's opinion.

Sophie dashed back to the row of cubbies. Mindy's was near the end. Mindy was pulling all her stuff out. Her best friend, Lily Lemley, was catching it.

"Don't worry, Mindy. It's got to be in there somewhere," Lily said.

"Oh, no, it doesn't," Mindy huffed. "My mother

told me some jealous girl might take it." She glared at the other kids. "And she was right."

Quickly, the whole class gathered around. Ms. Steele was busy writing on the board.

Sophie stepped up in front of Mindy. "This is a case for Sophie the Snoop if there ever was one!" she declared.

Mindy looked up at her with squinty eyes. Her lips got tight and pinched. "You! I saw the way you looked at my phone. Give it back!" She held out her hand.

"Huh? Who? Me?" Sophie shook her head. "I'm not the thief!" she said. She held up her magnifying glass. "I'm here to solve this mystery!"

Mindy leaned back. "Oh, yeah?" She cocked her head.

At the same time, Lily leaned forward. "Thanks, but no thanks, Sophie. We don't need your help," she said.

Sophie sighed.

Okay. Fine. It wasn't like she really wanted to help them. She was just jumping in because that was what detectives did. (And because maybe if she found the lip-gloss phone, Mindy would let her try it.)

But then Mindy frowned at Lily. "Speak for yourself," she said. "Go ahead, Sophie. Find it. And hurry! My lips are getting dry."

Sophie smiled with satisfaction. But she also had to roll her eyes. Snooping for snooty Mindy was not going to be an easy job.

"Okay. Everybody step away from the crime scene," she announced.

But just as she flipped open her notebook, Sophie heard another voice—Dean's.

"Hey! My trading cards! They were in my cubby. But now they're not!" he said.

Then Ben exclaimed, "Tweety! My Tweety Bird! He's gone!"

And so was Sophie A.'s brand-new chapter book.

And Grace's shiny new shoes. (They were the only shoes she'd worn since she'd gotten them. Except during gym. Then Grace changed into sneakers and left her new shoes in room 10.)

There was only one answer to these mysteries. And the answer made Sophie's heart race.

She looked around at her classmates. "I, Sophie the Snoop, suspect that a thief has been in our room!"

A few kids gasped.

"This is awful!" Sophie A. said.

Sophie nodded. She agreed...but she also thought it was great!

In fact, it was almost a snoop's dream come true. Sophie bet Sherlock Holmes never had so many mysteries to solve all at once!

"We should really tell Ms. Steele," Grace said calmly. She turned to the front of the room.

What?

"No!" Sophie gasped. "I can solve these mysteries all by myself!" What kind of snoop would she be if she asked a sub for help?

"Are you sure?" Ben asked. "I really need my Tweety back."

Sophie stood up very straight. "Sure, I'm sure," she said.

That was when Ms. Steele called, "Um...what's taking you all so long? Find your workbooks quickly. We, um, have a lot of work to get done."

Sophie grinned a big snoop grin.

And the world's biggest case to crack, too! she thought.

☆　　☆　　☆

Uh-oh.

Sophie had a problem. A big one.

The problem was that it was hard to crack the world's biggest case when a substitute teacher was watching you every second!

"Um...excuse me. But what are you doing?" Ms. Steele asked.

Sophie was crouched next to Mindy's cubby. She had rubber gloves on and held her magnifying glass in one hand. She had just covered Mindy's cubby with baby powder so she could dust for fingerprints. But something about the way Ms. Steele looked at her made Sophie say, "Nothing."

The rest of the students were doing their spelling. They all turned around. Mindy let out a small "Agh!" when she saw the baby powder all over her cubby. Everyone else just laughed.

"Well... it looks to me like you've made a big mess. Um... please clean it up and get back to work?" Ms. Steele said.

Sophie sighed and cleaned up the powder (or did the best she could). So much for finding fingerprints. Still, she did have some good evidence in her plastic bags.

She had one very curly blond hair. And a very long black one. And part of a wrapper from a blue crayon. And a bent paper clip. And one butterscotch Life Saver. Sophie was pretty sure it had never been licked. As soon as this case was closed, she might even think about eating it.

Sophie tiptoed back to her seat and tried to do a little work. But all she could think about was the mystery. (Well, that and how gross Toby was.)

She flipped open her notebook and wrote The Case of the Room 10 Thief.

Then she listed the clues she had so far. But they just didn't make sense!

At last, she put the tip of her pencil on her paper again. She pressed down hard. *Snap!* The tip broke off. Sophie slipped her notebook into her pocket. Then she stood up again.

"Um...what are you doing *now*?" Ms. Steele asked right away.

Sophie held up her pencil. She pointed toward the front of the room. "I'm going to the pencil sharpener," she coolly told the sub. *To see if the thief left any clues there!* she added in her head.

Sophie tiptoed across the room slowly. Her eyes darted all around. She watched her classmates working silently. Did one of them do it? Could one of them have done such a dastardly deed? Was this the beginning of a life of crime, maybe?

Suddenly, Sophie heard a sneeze. She turned.

Was it Kate? Did she have a code note for Sophie? Maybe she had some kind of lead!

But no. Kate made an "ew" face. She wiped her arm and scooted her chair back. The sneezer was Dean, sitting next to her. He closed his eyes and sneezed again.

Poor Kate. And her poor paper. It looked like it got wet.

Sophie's seat, next to Toby, was definitely the worst. But even though Dean was nice, it looked like Kate's seat was almost as bad.

And poor Sydney, Sophie thought as her eyes moved across the room. She had to sit next to Archie today. That was almost torture!

There was nothing nice about Archie, as far as Sophie could tell. He was loud and rude and he picked his nose. Plus he had that dirty-sock smell.

And not that it mattered, but he also stole friends.

Of course, Sophie didn't care about that.

Not much, that is.

A thought suddenly hit her. What if *Archie* was the thief?

Wow! Sophie started to smile. How great would that be?

Then she could tell Principal Tate. And he could kick Archie out of school. Then Archie could never pick on Sophie—or anybody else.

And he could never, ever go and steal another friend. . . .

Not that Sophie cared about that.

Not much, that is.

But a snoop had to work with the facts. Hopes were not enough, she knew. Sophie needed to make a list of suspects and their motives. ("Motives" was a word for "reasons," she was pretty sure.)

Sophie pulled out her notebook so she could write Archie's motives down. But—oh, yeah— she still had not sharpened her pencil. She could not write until she did. So she kept tiptoeing slowly toward the pencil sharpener and made a quick list in her head instead.

1) Archie would do anything to get Dean's trading cards. (Everyone knew that.)
2) He had threatened to take Ben's Tweety Bird lots and lots of times.
3) Plus nothing of Archie's was stolen. What about that!

Okay, maybe that wasn't a motive. But it sure was a fact. And facts didn't lie. They spoke for themselves!

On the other hand, there were Mindy's lipgloss phone, Grace's shoes, and Sophie A.'s book. Why would Archie want those?

He read only comics. And he never dressed up.

Oh, who cared? Maybe *why* wasn't important. There was another question, though. *How?* How had Archie stolen everything while they were at gym?

Sophie sighed. She needed more facts.

Archie's table was near the reading corner. Slowly, Sophie tiptoed toward it. As soon as she got to the bookcase, she crouched down and held her breath.

Sophie didn't move a muscle. She was like a statue (of a snoop!).

She leaned her ear against the big book Ms. Moffly had read to them about verbs. (*Hey!* she thought. *"Snoop" is a verb and a noun, too!*) Then Sophie listened as hard as she could.

"Stop looking at my paper, Archie. Or I'm going to tell," Sophie heard Sydney say.

Aha! Archie was a cheater, cheater, pumpkin eater. More proof that he was a thief!

"I'm not looking at your paper," Archie said back. "I'm just looking at the spider crawling over it."

"Aghhhh!" Sydney screamed.

Archie laughed. "Gotcha!"

The rest of the class started laughing, too.

"Um...quiet. Everyone. Right now," Ms. Steele said. "Do I need to separate you two?" she asked Sydney and Archie.

"Yes!" they both said.

"Okay...um...then I will?" Ms. Steele said.

Sophie heard the sub get up and walk—*clack, clack, clack*—across the room.

"Um...Cindy? Please switch seats with Sydney?" Ms. Steele said.

"Who? Me?" That was Mindy.

This time Sophie laughed.

Oops. She shouldn't have.

The next thing Sophie knew, the sub was leaning over her. "What are you doing *now*?" asked Ms. Steele.

"Uh . . ." Sophie tried to think. "I dropped my pencil?" she said, looking up.

She did not expect to see the sub smile. (After all, she hadn't smiled all day.) But it sure looked like Ms. Steele was smiling now. Halfway, at least.

But that was not what surprised Sophie. That was not what made her eyes pop.

What *really* surprised Sophie was the way

Ms. Steele's lips looked. They were pink and shiny...like she had put on lip gloss!

Lip gloss. Just like Mindy's.

Sophie's mouth fell open.

Archie wasn't the thief.

Ms. Steele was!

CHAPTER 6

It all made perfect sense! It was even right there in her name!

No one had ever been robbed in room 10 until Ms. *Steal* showed up. That was why the sub was so nervous—because she was up to no good!

Why hadn't Sophie made her a suspect before?

Sophie wondered if this was the first time Ms. Steele had ever robbed a school. Or did she do it all the time? Maybe she was on the FBI's Most Wanted list and no one even knew! Maybe she even *poisoned* teachers so she could come rob their rooms!

Poor Ms. Moffly. If she was poisoned, Sophie hoped there was an antidote.

She also hoped that cracking this case would make her even more famous than Sherlock Holmes!

Sophie was careful to keep her eyes down as she went back to her seat. She was sure that if Ms. Steele saw them, she would know that Sophie was onto her. And Sophie wasn't ready for that. She had to tell Kate first!

She sat down at her table to write a note—in code, of course.

But wait! She still had not sharpened her pencil. The tip was still broken off.

Great.

Now she was stuck.

Sophie couldn't get up *again* . . . but she couldn't keep this news all to herself, either. Sophie looked sideways at Toby. He might have an extra pencil she could use. She hated to ask. But she guessed she had to.

"Uh... Toby?" she said.

Then she stopped. This was hard. Sophie had not asked Toby for anything in a long time—except to mind his own business, that is. But that did not count.

"What?" Toby said. His face had a "why are you even talking to me?" look all over it. Then he grinned and asked her a question. "Hey, have you solved any of those mysteries yet?"

That surprised Sophie a lot. Almost as much as Ms. Steele's shiny lips.

Then she frowned. Toby was teasing her. He probably thought she was not even close to solving the thefts yet.

Well, she had news for him!

"As a matter of fact, I have solved them," she said. She crossed her arms.

"Really?" Toby's eyes got big.

Sophie smiled. "They don't call me Sophie the Snoop for nothing, you know."

Toby kept staring at her, like he was waiting

for her to say more. But Sophie was not about to tell him what she'd found out. Kate had to be the first to know.

"So?" he said finally.

"So," she said back. "So can I borrow a pencil?"

"That's it? A pencil?" Toby asked.

Sophie nodded. "Yes."

What did he think she was going to say?

"Don't worry. I'll give it back," she told him.

Toby handed her a freshly sharpened yellow pencil. "Keep it." He shrugged.

Really?

"Thanks," Sophie said, shocked. She tried hard to keep her eyebrows from shooting up.

Was Toby being nice? For the first time all year?

"Now that it's got your cooties all over it, I don't want it," Toby added.

Sophie rolled her eyes. No. He was the same old pain in the neck. Sometimes she could not believe that Toby used to be her friend.

But at least she had a pencil now. She turned back to her paper and began to write with it.

20 8 5 / 20 8 9 5 6 / 9 19 / 13 19. / 19 20 5 5 12 5!

After a few minutes — and some erasing — she finished the note. Done! She grinned and folded it tight. Then she put it on the edge of the table and fake sneezed with all her might: *"A-CHOO!"*

Eve and Sydney were sitting nearby. They both turned and said, "Bless you."

"Uh, thanks," Sophie told them. If only Kate had heard her, too. But no, she did not seem to.

So Sophie sneezed again.

And again.

And again.

"A-CHOO!"

"AAA-CHOOOO!!!"

Eve and Sydney looked at her funny.

Toby leaned away. "You'd better not sneeze on me like Dean did!" he said.

Sophie groaned. There was too much sneezing in this class.

Maybe the owl sound would get Kate's attention, even if it did sound weird.

Sophie hooted. *"Whoo! Whoo!"*

Kate looked over.

Yes!

Kate winked and got up to sharpen her pencil. She took the long way, past Sophie's desk. She picked up the note as she walked by. Back at her own table, she opened it.

Sophie watched. It took Kate a whole minute to decode what it said:

The thief is Ms. Steele!

At last, Kate got it. She looked up. Her eyes were round. Her mouth shaped the word "Really?"

Sophie nodded hard.

Then Kate bent over the paper. She checked her code key and wrote something down. But Sophie couldn't get up and grab the note until it was time to put their spelling workbooks away. *Ugh!*

Finally, back at her table, Sophie read it.

$$25\ 15\ 21\ /\ 8\ 1\ 22\ 5\ /\ 20\ 15\ /$$
$$20\ 5\ 12\ 12\ /\ 20\ 8\ 5\ /\ 16\ 18\ 9\ 14\ 3\ 9\ 16\ 1\ 12!$$

She hurried to check her code key.

You have to tell the pahinciafaab!

Pahinciafaab? What was that?

Sophie tried to read it again.

You have to tell the prinadcipb!

Sophie sighed and scratched her head.

Then Toby leaned over. "What do you have to tell the principal?" he asked.

Sophie turned to him and glared. "Hey! That's a secret code. You can't read it," she said.

(Still, at the same time, she was kind of glad he did.)

And Kate was very right. Principal Tate had to be told. And who had to tell him? Sophie the Snoop!

Sophie could just see it. He would be so proud! He might even make her the official Snoop of the School! With her own desk. In the school office. Wouldn't that be cool?

But then Sophie thought of something else. What if Ms. Steele denied the whole thing? What if she lied and said she was innocent? (She was a criminal, after all.) If she did, Sophie would probably need even more proof.

Just then, Ms. Steele spoke up. "Um . . . attention, please. It's, um, time for lunch?"

Lunch! Sophie had almost forgotten. The class lined up.

Then, suddenly, a thought hit her. A big one! As soon as they all left, Ms. Steele would be alone in the room again. She could steal more stuff. She might even try to escape with all the stolen loot!

Sophie could not let that happen. She knew what she had to do. She had to stay in the classroom. She had to snoop on Ms. Steele!

Besides, it was Meat Loaf Day. Sophie did not mind missing that too much.

So instead of lining up for the lunchroom, Sophie whispered to Kate, "I'm going under-cover!" Then she slipped on her 3-D glasses. (Who knew? They might help.)

Sophie ducked behind the open classroom door. There! Her trap was set.

It would have been the perfect place to snoop from, Sophie was sure. Except for one thing: As soon as the class left, the sub closed the door.

"Sophie! What are you doing *now*?" Ms. Steele said.

CHAPTER 7

Sophie peered up, through her 3-D glasses, into the eyes of Ms. Steele. She had never looked at the eyes of a thief before! It made her heart beat very fast. She quickly bent her head to stare at the shoes of the thief instead.

"Sophie, why didn't you go to lunch with the rest of the class?" Ms. Steele asked.

Why? Sophie bit her lip. She could not tell the sub the truth. And she also couldn't pretend that she was just being slow. If she went to lunch now, she'd be leaving a thief there alone!

No. Sophie had to stay.

So she swallowed hard and looked back up. "Can I stay here, Ms. Steele . . . with you?"

"Here?" Ms. Steele sounded surprised.

I've foiled her plans! Sophie thought.

"Please," Sophie begged. "It would be such a great chance . . ." She tried to think. ". . . to do extra reading!" she finished.

Ms. Steele chewed on her fingernail. *Suspicious behavior!* Sophie thought.

"Um, well, okay," Ms. Steele said. "I was just going to eat my lunch here, myself." She shrugged. "But if I were you, I wouldn't try to read with those glasses on," she said.

The sub returned to her desk and Sophie sighed with relief. That had been very quick snoop thinking, if she did say so herself.

Sophie sat down at her table and slipped her glasses off. Then she nibbled on her sandwich and took out her chapter book. She opened it and held it up in front of her face. But did she read it? Nope. She did not.

What she did was watch the sub. She watched

her very carefully. But Ms. Steele did not do much. She just took out her lunch from a green bag behind her desk.

A *big* green bag, Sophie noticed. Big enough to hold all kinds of stolen stuff!

Then, with a smile at Sophie, Ms. Steele took out a book, too.

Sophie wondered if just maybe it was Sophie A.'s missing book....

But nope.

Sophie squinted to read the title: *The Cat Who Robbed a Bank.*

Hmm. She had two thoughts. One: That was just the kind of thing a thief would read. And two: It sounded good.

But maybe, just maybe, the sub was only *pretending* to read. Of course! Ms. Steele was probably watching Sophie—and waiting for a chance to steal *more* stuff. Sophie could not help smiling. She was stopping more crimes from being done.

Then again, Sophie kind of wanted the sub to

steal more stuff. Then Sophie could catch her dead-handed! (Or was it *red*-handed? She wasn't sure.)

That was when Sophie decided it was time to set a trap.

She had brought her backpack to her desk for lunch. She took out her detective hat and put it on the floor. She pushed it into the aisle very slowly with her foot. Then she crumpled up her brown paper lunch bag. She waved it as she stood.

"Oh, Ms. Steeeeele!" she called. "I'm going to throw this away. And go all the way over there—to the sink—to get a drink."

The sub looked up and smiled. "Okay, Sophie."

Sophie turned and tiptoed away, humming softly. Then she stopped and spun around. She was sure she'd see Ms. Steele standing up. But the sub was still sitting down.

Sophie tiptoed a little more, then turned. Then tiptoed. Then turned. Then stopped. She had reached the sink. Still nothing. She bent to take a drink and sighed.

She kept peering over her shoulder as the cold water dribbled down her chin.

Come on, Ms. Steele! she thought. *Take my hat. I know you want it!*

All of a sudden, her patience paid off. Ms. Steele got up and walked toward Sophie's hat, just as she'd hoped.

Sophie held her breath. She watched the sub bend over and scoop the hat right up.

Then Sophie bolted across the room. "Gotcha!" she called.

"Excuse me?" said Ms. Steele. The sub stared at Sophie's finger. It was pointing at her. "This is your hat, isn't it?" she asked. "I just found it on the floor. You really shouldn't leave it there. You should hang it on your cubby hook."

Huh?

Sophie dropped her finger. This was not her plan at all. Ms. Steele was way too sneaky! (Or

else she did not like Sophie's hat enough to really steal it.)

"Thanks," Sophie mumbled. She took the hat and hung it up.

She guessed it was time for Plan B. If only she knew what Plan B was.

If I could just get Ms. Steele's bag, Sophie thought, *and take it to Principal Tate . . .*

And right then, as if he'd heard her thoughts, the principal appeared in the doorway. Sophie couldn't believe it!

"Hello there, Ms. Steele," he said. "Just checking in." His eyes fell on Sophie. "Why, Miss Miller. This is a surprise!" Principal Tate looked back at the substitute. "Is this a punishment?"

"Oh. Um, no. Not at all, Mr. Tate." Ms. Steele shook her head very fast. "Sophie just wanted to do some extra reading."

Principal Tate turned to Sophie. One eyebrow was up, and one was down. "Extra reading?" He looked confused. But that was okay. Sophie knew that it would all make sense as soon as she turned the substitute in. "Well, I'm sure Ms. Moffly would be very proud," he went on. Then Principal Tate turned back to the sub. "Ms. Steele, could we have a word in the hall?"

Ms. Steele looked more nervous than ever as she followed the principal out of the room and closed the door.

Poor Ms. Steele. Sophie almost felt sorry for her. But no! What was she thinking? Sophie tossed that thought away fast.

Then she got a new one. This was Sophie's chance to get the sub's bag full of loot and give it to Principal Tate!

Sophie didn't waste a second. She tiptoed—fast—up to the teacher's desk.

She bent down beside the big green bag. It was open. Yes! Of course, Sophie knew she'd see Ben's Tweety Bird, Dean's cards, and Grace's shoes. She was sure she'd find Mindy's lip-gloss phone and Sophie A.'s chapter book, too.

And who knew? There might be more stuff. Stuff no one had even realized was gone yet.

But Sophie didn't see those things when she looked inside the bag. All she saw were:

- a folded-up newspaper—with a crossword puzzle half done
- a big red wallet
- a silver travel mug
- some keys on a keychain that said "I (heart) cats"
- a pack of minty chewing gum
- a tube of plain old lipstick

Sophie couldn't believe it. Where was all the stolen stuff? This was even more of a mystery than she'd thought.

That's when she spied something else, down at the bottom of the bag. . . .

Was it? Yes!

A phone!

And it was *pink*!

Sophie had to do it. She reached in. And she pulled it out.

Then she sighed one of the biggest sighs she'd ever sighed in her whole life.

It wasn't Mindy's lip-gloss phone. It was a *real* cell phone.

Aw! Too bad!

She started to put the phone back into the bag. Then suddenly, she jumped. The phone began playing a song. And a man's picture popped up on the screen.

The real phone was ringing!

What do I do? Sophie thought. *What would a snoop do?*

She knew that a snoop would answer the phone So that's what she did (in a disguised voice, of course).

Sophie punched the "talk" button. "Er...hello?" she said, very low.

"Hi...Sophie?" a man's voice replied.

Sophie felt her stomach flip-flop. "Um, yes — I mean, *no!*" she said. "I mean...how did you know?"

"Isn't this your phone?" asked the man. "Are you okay, Sophie? Do you have a cold?"

Suddenly, Sophie realized something. Ms. Steele's name was Sophie, too!

"Um . . ." She tried to think quickly. "Actually, *that* Sophie is busy right now. Can I take a message?" she asked.

The man paused. At last, he said, "Sure. Just tell her good luck."

Then he said good-bye and the phone went dead.

Sophie's heart began to thump.

Good luck?

That was bad!

So! The Case of the Room 10 Thief had taken a turn. Ms. Steele *was* the thief. But she was not working alone!

This was even bigger than Sophie had thought. She had to tell Principal Tate right away! But before she could even move, the classroom door opened.

There stood Ms. Steele—the thief!—with Principal Tate. But that wasn't all. The rest of the class was there, too, back from lunch.

They were all looking at her. And most of their eyes were wide.

"Sophie! What are you doing with my phone?" Ms. Steele cried.

CHAPTER 8

The next thing Sophie knew, she was in the school office—with Principal Tate.

She had planned to go to him, but not exactly like this. Somehow, Sophie had ended up standing there like *she* was the thief.

"I must say, Miss Miller, I am very surprised," the principal said, shaking his head. "What do you have to say for yourself?"

Sophie stood in front of his desk very calmly. It would all be okay just as soon as she explained.

She took a deep breath. "I am not the thief, Principal Tate," she said. "The *substitute* is!"

The principal lifted one eyebrow, then the other. (He was good at that.) Then he leaned forward on his elbows. "Now, *this* is even more surprising. What in the world makes you say that?" he asked.

"Well . . ." Sophie bit her lip. Where should she begin? "For one thing, all this stuff was stolen today—the day that Ms. Steele is here. So it's pretty elementary, don't you think?" she said.

"But your classmates seem to think that *you* did it, to be some kind of snoop," the principal said, looking at her closely. "And the fact is, *you* were the one caught holding Ms. Steele's phone."

Me? The thief? Never! Sophie felt her face get hot.

"Me? The thief? Never!" She crossed her heart. "I swear! I'm not the one who got a phone call telling me good luck with my robbery! Don't you think that's suspicious? Plus she reads books about cats who rob banks!" Sophie paused to take a breath. "And her name is Ms. *Steele!*"

78

She crossed her arms. He could not argue with that!

"I bet she robs schools all the time, Principal Tate," she told him. "You should probably call all your principal friends and see if they're missing anything."

"Sophie, Sophie, Sophie." The principal shook his head.

Uh-oh, Sophie thought. *Was that good? Or very bad?* The principal never used first names. And now he was using hers. Three times. In a row.

"I would be surprised to learn that Ms. Steele leads a life of crime," Principal Tate said. "As far as I know, she's working hard to earn her teaching degree. And this is her first day substituting." He sighed. "Ever."

"Well, that's even better!" Sophie told him. She grinned. "Good thing I was in her class! I showed her that she can't get away with robbing kids. And the judge might be easy on her if it's just her first time. Do you want to call in the police now? Or should I?"

The principal opened his mouth. But there was a knock at the door before anything came out.

"Come in," said Principal Tate.

The door opened. There was Ms. Steele . . . and Toby. *What's* he *doing here?* Sophie wondered.

"Um . . . this young man has something to tell you, Mr. Tate," Ms. Steele said.

Sophie felt her jaw drop. She tried to close it. But she could not. This was just like Toby to try to get her in more trouble!

Sophie glared at him and thought hard about sticking out her tongue.

Then Toby took a deep breath and said, "I'm sorry. I took all the stuff."

Huh?

Now Sophie was really confused.

Ms. Steele *wasn't* the thief? But Sophie had been so sure!

And Toby *was* the thief? Wow! That surprised even her.

But not as much as the feeling she suddenly got. She felt bad for Toby. He was going to be in

big trouble. She started to wish she hadn't told Principal Tate to call the cops.

Of course, Sophie was also mad. But not at Toby. At herself. What kind of snoop could be so wrong about so much?

The principal looked mad, too. "Mr. Myers, this is very serious," he said.

Ms. Steele put a hand on Toby's shoulder. "Why don't you explain?" she said to him.

Toby looked at Sophie—and looked away fast. "I wasn't going to steal the stuff and *keep* it," he said.

"Then why did you do it?" Principal Tate asked.

"To help *her*," Toby said quietly. He nodded at Sophie. She almost gasped.

Help her? *How?* Sophie had to hear this.

By then, Toby's face was so red his freckles had almost disappeared.

He took another breath. "She was just so crazy to solve mysteries," he went on. "She even had a detective hat. But there weren't any mysteries.

So I thought I'd make some up." Toby shrugged and looked down at the floor. "And it was so easy to take the stuff while everyone was lining up for gym. It's all in my backpack. I was going to return it, really. I mean, if Sophie the *Snoop* didn't find it first."

Sophie was speechless. But a zillion thoughts zipped through her head.

Thoughts like *What?* And *Really?* And *Sorry, Ms. Steele. . . .*

Sophie had snooped around in the substitute's bag for nothing. And missed lunch, too.

And speaking of missing, how had she missed Toby's taking all that stuff? She guessed it was because she had not wanted to look at him much.

What was Toby thinking? She made herself look at him just to see. But his face was down. He was looking at his feet.

So she looked at his red head and wondered, *Why did he do what he did?*

Was it really because he liked the name Sophie

the Snoop and wanted to help her earn it? Or was he just saying that to get out of trouble? Was he trying to prove she *couldn't* really solve mysteries? Was he just being mean?

That, for sure, was the biggest mystery!

CHAPTER 9

A few minutes later, Sophie was glad to be out of the principal's office.

But she was not glad to be back in room 10. Everyone — except Kate — was talking about all the trouble she was in!

Of course, they weren't just talking about her. They were talking about Toby, too. He'd given everything back and he'd explained what he'd done.

Archie thought it was hilarious. "Why didn't you tell me?" he asked him.

"Tweety!" said Ben. He gave his Tweety Bird a hug.

Mindy was furious. "Don't you ever touch my lip-gloss phone again!" she fumed. She inspected it for damage. Then she quickly dabbed on some lip gloss.

Sophie, meanwhile, slunk back to her seat. The one next to Toby. (As if things weren't bad enough.) She really, really wished she could ask to move. But she could not even look at Ms. Steele. How could she speak to her?

Sophie felt awful for making the sub's first day of teaching so hard. She should have known better. How could someone named Sophie be bad, after all?

Sophie guessed that she was not as much of a snoop as she had thought. She was still just plain old boring Sophie the *Nothing*. As usual.

The good news was that it was almost time for art class with her very favorite teacher, Ms. Bart. So Sophie did not have to stay in her seat next to Toby for long. Art could not come soon enough.

She hoped they would do clay. She felt like squeezing stuff in her hands. Or maybe splatter painting. Sophie could really get into that.

Something—anything—to take her mind off Sophie the Snoop.

But when Sophie got to the art room, she saw that there was a little mirror at each of their seats.

Mindy picked hers up. Sophie rolled her eyes as Mindy blew herself a kiss.

Then Ms. Bart called for their attention. She had her hair in two long, long braids. One had glitter stuck to it. The other looked like it had been dipped in purple paint.

"Hey, everyone," Ms. Bart said. "Today we're doing something really cool. We're going to draw self-portraits. That means *you* draw a picture of *you*!"

Really?

Sophie looked around. Everyone else—especially Mindy—seemed to think that it was a great idea. But drawing a picture of herself was the *last* thing Sophie wanted to do just then.

Kate reached for a pencil and quickly drew something round.

"Aren't you going to look at yourself first?" Sophie asked.

Kate grinned and shrugged. "Well, I know I have a *head*," she replied.

Sophie picked up her mirror. She studied her face. It frowned back. She grabbed a pencil and started to draw, then stopped. *Blah!* It wasn't right.

Sophie knew that she was not a great artist. No, Sophie the Artist would never be her name. (Sydney and Eve were the best in her class. And Jack, too, if you counted cartoons.) But she loved to sculpt. And draw. And paint. She especially loved to glue stuff. What did Ms. Bart call that? Oh, right. Collage.

But Kate wasn't a great artist, either, and she was doing okay with her self-portrait.

And Lily was almost finished. Her self-portrait looked a lot more like *Mindy* than herself. Sophie wasn't surprised.

Still, that was better than nothing at all. Nothing at all was what Sophie had.

She tried again. And again. But after twenty minutes, all she had was a paper full of gray smudges. And a lapful of eraser dust.

For the first time ever in art class, Sophie was not having fun.

"Sophie, how are you doing?" Ms. Bart asked as she walked up. She knelt down and looked at Sophie's blank paper, then at Sophie. "What's up?"

"I can't do it," Sophie said glumly. "I mean, I know what I *should* look like. But when I try to draw it, it comes out wrong."

Ms. Bart put her hand on Sophie's shoulder. "It doesn't have to be perfect," she said.

"But if it doesn't look just like me, what's the point?" Sophie asked.

Ms. Bart smiled. "Come here. Let me show you something."

She stood up and Sophie followed her to a bulletin board covered with art. Some looked like a real artist had made it. And some did not.

Ms. Bart pointed to a painting of a man. He had one big black eye and one small one. And a very giant nose. "This is a self-portrait by Pablo Picasso—one of the greatest artists in the world," she said.

Then she pointed to another. "And this is by the artist Marc Chagall." It showed an artist painting in a bow tie. His skin was blue. And his hair was green. But those were not the strangest things in the picture.

"He has a lot of fingers!" Sophie told Ms. Bart.

The art teacher grinned. "Really, he had just five on each hand, like you and me. But he *chose* to paint more"

He chose to? Really?

"You don't think he lost count? Or messed up?" Sophie asked.

Ms. Bart laughed. "Maybe, Sophie. But that's what I mean. These artists didn't care if their paintings looked *exactly* like them. The paintings showed how they felt. In here." She pointed to her smock, just above her heart. "You can always take a picture of the outside with a camera. But a drawing can show what's inside. Don't you think that's the best part?"

Yeah, maybe. (Unless you were Mindy VonBoffmann. Her outsides were much better than her insides, in Sophie's opinion.)

But Sophie didn't see how this solved her problem at all. "So how do I show what's inside?" she asked Ms. Bart. "I can *see* the outside, and I can't even draw that!"

Ms. Bart squeezed her shoulder. "It'll come. Just relax."

Sophie sighed and looked back at the portraits on the wall. Then she noticed another one. It had every color of the rainbow in it. It was hard to tell exactly what the person looked like. But Sophie could see that she had long hair, and she was happy, and it would be easy to be her friend.

Sophie turned from the picture to Ms. Bart.

"Is that you?" she asked.

Ms. Bart grinned. "It sure is!"

Sophie headed back to her table. Kate was

almost done with her self-portrait. She was adding freckles. "What do you think?" she asked. "Too much?"

Sophie grinned and shook her head. "No. Definitely not."

Kate had made her hair a little wilder than it really was. And her eyes were kind of far from her triangle nose. But her smile was so big you hardly noticed at all.

Sophie picked up her pencil and thought about how she felt inside. She leaned over her paper and she started to draw.

Ms. Bart came over later, just as she was finishing.

"Sophie," she said. "That's wonderful! I can't wait to hang it up."

Sophie smiled. It wasn't perfect. Her ears looked like seashells. And her bangs were way too short. But she liked the way her smile curled up just enough. And her long eyelashes made her light brown eyes stand out.

Some kids had just drawn a face. But Sophie

drew a shirt, too. Not the plain red one she was wearing. No. This shirt was green, and it had a rainbow heart in the middle that got bigger the more she drew. Her smile was not as big as Kate's. But it showed lots of teeth (and a space for the one she had lost recently).

In fact, the more she looked at her portrait, the more proud Sophie felt. But she wasn't sure she wanted it hung up.

"Is it okay if I take it with me?" she asked Ms. Bart.

The art teacher nodded. "Oh, yes!" she said. "Of course!"

Sophie had one more thing to add. It was the most important part—a big speech bubble. Because her feelings had something to say to someone.

CHAPTER 10

$\mathcal{B}$ack in room 10, after art, Sophie walked up to Ms. Steele.

She swallowed. Two times. And she handed the sub her self-portrait.

"For me?" Ms. Steele asked. She gently took it. And something happened to her eyes. They got crinkly at the corners. Sophie got a little worried. Then she saw that it was part of a big smile.

The sub looked down at Sophie's picture and read the words:

I am sorry I snooped in your stuff.
I hope you sub for us again.
I have a message for you, too:
"Good luck, Sophie Steele."

Ms. Steele's eyes moved to Sophie. "Thank you so much, Sophie. This means a lot."

Sophie sighed. She felt much better. It was good to have those feelings out.

But she was still feeling other things. They quickly filled her insides up.

She still felt sorry that her snooping had gone so wrong. She had thought she was a natural snoop. Now she guessed that she was not.

And she felt mixed up about Toby. Was he really being mean? Had he been trying to make her look silly when he'd faked those mysteries? Or maybe he didn't hate her as much as she thought. Maybe he was trying to help her be Sophie the Snoop after all.

It was so hard to know!

She went back to her seat—the one next to Toby.

I should have asked the sub if I could move, Sophie thought.

She checked the clock. It was almost three. *Phew.* Any minute, the bell would ring. Then she could get up and go.

But maybe, just maybe, she should take this chance. Maybe she should say something to Toby. Maybe she should even thank him.

But how?

Well, there was one way. Sophie swallowed—hard.

"Thank you, Toby," she said very, very softly.

Toby's head was down. He'd been pulling rubber off the edge of his shoe. Slowly, he looked up.

"For what?" he asked her.

"Uh..." Sophie bit her lip. Her mind was suddenly blank. What should she say next?

"For getting us both in big trouble today"?

No. That was no good. "For trying to help me be Sophie the Snoop"?

But Toby was looking at her so funny Sophie wished she'd kept her mouth shut.

"Uh, for letting me borrow your pencil. Even if I did get cooties on it," she mumbled.

"Oh, that." Toby shrugged. But then he also grinned a little.

Wow. They were almost having a conversation!

And then the bell rang.

Ms. Steele stood up.

"Good-bye, class," she said. "It's been a . . . um . . . very memorable day."

Sophie got up along with the rest of the class. Then she turned back to Toby. There were suddenly things she wanted to ask. Did he even know she was playing soccer now? And had he gotten a new dog yet?

But the next thing she knew, Archie was standing next to them. And that wasn't all. He had her Sherlock Holmes hat!

"Hey, that's my hat! Hand it over!" Sophie cried.

Archie stuck out his tongue. "Make me!" He laughed.

Sophie glared and tried to grab the hat. But Archie was too quick.

"Hey, Arch!" she heard Toby say. "Pass it. Over here!"

Sophie turned to see Toby waving. She did not know what she was more full of—surprise or happiness.

Archie didn't know that Toby was on her side again! She watched Archie toss Toby the hat. And she crossed her arms and grinned. She held one hand out and waited for Toby to give her the hat.

Then... *what?*

Sophie couldn't believe it. Toby took the hat and ran out of the room instead!

How could she, Sophie Miller, have been so dumb? Toby Myers had not changed. Not one little bit!

Sophie chased him into the hall and all the way outside, with Archie close behind. "Give it back, right now! It's not even my hat. It's my dad's," she called.

"Then he'll have to make me," Toby shouted back. "Here, Archie! Catch!"

Ugh! Inside, Sophie groaned. If there was one game she really disliked, it was keep-away. She hated it so much!

"I'm not kidding, guys," she yelled. "Give it back!"

By then, the whole class had gathered around.

"You know, the substitute is coming," Grace warned them.

Archie shrugged. "Oh, all right," he said to Sophie. "Have your hat back. Here."

He started to hand it to Sophie. But then he stopped and did something terrible—something that made the whole class go, "Oh, no!"

Archie held up her hat and he *licked* it.

Ew! Gross! Sophie thought.

She took the hat with two fingers. She didn't know what else to do. She held it very far away from her. And she wrinkled up her nose.

"Put it on. I *dare* you," Archie said. He laughed and gave Toby a high five.

Sophie's nose unwrinkled. She glared her fiercest glare. Had Archie just *dared* her?

How dare he do that!

She looked at the poor hat, all cootied up with Archie's spit. She did not want to wear it. But now she *had* to.

Sophie closed her eyes and took a deep breath. Then she set the hat on her head.

"Whoa!" her friends gasped.

"Wow! You really did it," Kate said beside her. She was impressed.

Sophie shrugged. "Well, he dared me, didn't he? There's never been a dare I wouldn't do...." Then suddenly, she smiled. She was getting an idea! "Hey, Kate! Maybe *that's* it!"

Kate grabbed her hand. She waggled her eyebrows and grinned. "Come on, Sophie the *Daredevil*!" she said. "Let's go home and wash that hat!"

Does Sophie dare to
try out a new name?

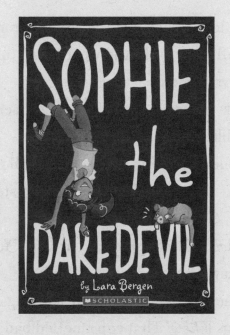

Take a peek at Sophie's next adventure....

Sophie looked down at the cup in front of her. It was full. Very full. And what it was full of did not look very good.

"Drink it!" said Jack. He leaned across the lunch table. "Go ahead. I *dare* you!"

The other kids from her class were all gathered around. "Drink it! Drink it!" they started to chant.

"I will, I will," Sophie said at last. "You know there's never been a dare I wouldn't do."

But she also couldn't help leaning back in her chair. *Whew!* That cup smelled bad!

It pretty much smelled like what was in it. And by themselves, those things were okay. Sophie liked milk. And fruit punch. And chocolate pudding. And ketchup. And applesauce. And ranch dressing. And chicken noodle soup.

But together?

Not so much.

But Sophie had asked for it. Or she had asked for a dare, anyway. How else would she prove her great new name?

Sophie the Daredevil! How good did that sound? How special! And unique! Sophie was dying for a name that would make her stand out. And now at last she'd found it!

In her head, she had ideas of what some extra-fun dares would be. Dares like climbing up the big oak tree. Or jumping off the swing. Or holding her breath for a whole minute. (She'd even practiced that.)

Unfortunately, things had not gone as she planned. Sophie's friends were happy to dare her. Very happy. But their ideas of dares were . . . different.

They were GROSS.

All of them.

So far, Sophie had licked the blacktop *and* the window on the school bus.

She had smelled Dean's sneakers (both of them!), and sat on a mysterious wet spot.

Then there was the lunchroom. That was not fun at all. This "Drink of Doom" was actually Sophie's second one.

Sophie looked down at the lumpy liquid. A noodle floated to the top.

"Drink it! Drink it! Drink it!" her friends chanted.

Sophie's best friend, Kate, patted her back. "Just close your eyes and pretend it's a smoothie. Like the last time," she said.

"Right." Sophie made a face. She swallowed hard.

She wondered if she'd ever drink a smoothie again. Probably only if someone dared her. She would have to then.

At last, she sat up straight. She grabbed the

cup in one hand. She pinched her nose using the other and squeezed her eyes shut.

Gulp . . . gulp . . . gulp. Sophie let the liquid slosh down her throat.

Ugh! She did not feel good.

For a second she thought, *Was it worth it?*

Then a cheer rang out: "Yeah! Sophie!"

She smiled a big smile. *Was it worth it? Yes! For sure!*

KITTY CORNER

Where kitties get the love they need

 These purr-fect kittens need a home!

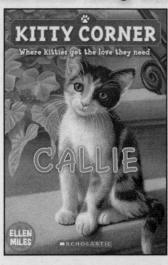

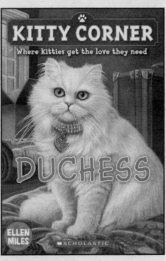